THE BEST EVER JOBS

JOBS IN MATH

ROB COLSON

PowerKiDS press
NEW YORK

Published in 2023 by The Rosen Publishing Group, Inc.
29 East 21st Street, New York, NY 10010

Series editor: Amy Pimperton
Produced by Tall Tree Ltd
Editor: Lara Murphy
Designer: Gary Hyde

Copyright © 2023 Wayland, a division of Hachette Children's Group

Cataloging-in-Publication Data
Names: Colson, Rob.
Title: Jobs in math / Rob Colson.
Description: New York : PowerKids Press, 2023. | Series: The best ever jobs | Includes glossary and index.
Identifiers: ISBN 9781725339163 (pbk.) | ISBN 9781725339170 (library bound) | ISBN 9781725339187 (ebook)
Subjects: LCSH: Mathematics--Vocational guidance--Juvenile literature.
Classification: LCC QA10.5 C647 2023 | DDC 510.23--dc23

Picture Credits
t-top, b-bottom, l-left, r-right, c-centre, fc-front cover, bc-back cover
3tr and 25t shutterstock/Multigon, 3rt and 38c shutterstock/Panda Vector, 3r, 5tl and 10l shutterstock/Colorlife, 3b shutterstock/Fireofheart, 4b shutterstock/pupunkkop, 5r shutterstock/bsd, 6b shutterstock/Yoko Design, 7t shutterstock/Jemastock, 7b Antoine Claudet, 8br shutterstock/bsd, 8b shutterstock/Laura Reyero, 8cr shutterstock/ArtHead, 9t unknown, 9b shutterstock/ylq, 10b shutterstock/yuRomanovich, 11t shutterstock/lavizzara, 12b shutterstock/ditttmer, 13t shutterstock/I.Noyan Yilmaz, 13b shutterstock/Mesa Studios, 14b shutterstock/Senoldo, 15t shutterstock/REDPIXEL.PL, 15b shutterstock/Yonhap/EPA, 16l shutterstock/a Sk, 17c shutterstock/karpenko_ilia, 18bl shutterstock/Pavel K, 18l and 18b shutterstock/Svetlana Avv, 19t Gary He, 19b and 39r shutterstock/Anatolir, 20l and 21c shutterstock/melazerg, 20r shutterstock/Vizualbyte, 21t shutterstock/Dan Kosmayer, 21b shutterstock/Line - design, 22l shutterstock/MitchGunn, 22r and 23b shutterstock/animicsgo, 23t shutterstock/mipan, 23b shutterstock/Bill Florence, 24l shutterstock/Apostle, 25b shutterstock/Jeff Chiu/AP, 26 shutterstock/Gorodenkoff, 27t and 27r NASA, 27b shutterstock/Ksenya Savva, 28–29b shutterstock/CataVic, 29t shutterstock/photocritical,
29r shutterstock/Maxim M, 30c shutterstock/Alhovik, 30r, 31b shutterstock/LYekaterina, 30b shutterstock/Roschetzky Photography, 31c shutterstock/rob zs, 32cl shutterstock/Valery Brozhinsky, 32b shutterstock/muuraa, 33t shutterstock/Susan Walsh/AP, 33b shutterstock/Svitlana Varfolomieieva, 34c shutterstock/lukmanhakim, 35t shutterstock/peiyang, 35b Strebe, 36cr and 48b shutterstock/Drekhann, 36b shutterstock/DGIM studio, 37t shutterstock/Naeblys, 37b NASA/Adam Cuerdon, 38b shutterstock/cherezoff, 39b Magnus Manske, 42c shutterstock/FrameStockFootages, 43tr shutterstock/josep perianes jorba, 43b shutterstock/TK Kurikawa, 44b shutterstocl/Daviel Krason, 45t shutterstock/Bornfree, 45tr shutterstock/Makalo86, 45c shutterstock/Sable Vector.

Every attempt has been made to clear copyright. Should there be any inadvertent omission, please apply to the publisher for rectification. The facts, dates and statistics in this book were correct at the time of printing.

Manufactured in the United States of America

CPSIA Compliance Information: Batch #CSPK23. For further information contact Rosen Publishing, New York, New York at 1-800-237-9932.
Find us on

Contents

Top math jobs	4
Computer programmer	6
Cryptographer	8
Meteorologist	10
Behind the scenes: Climate scientists	12
Research mathematician	14
Statistician	16
Opinion pollster	18
Sports analyst	20
Behind the scenes: Hawk-Eye	22
Roboticist	24
Behind the scenes: Robotics lab	26
Theme park designer	28
Urban planner	30
Fraud investigator	32
Cartographer	34
Space scientist	36
Astronomer	38
Behind the scenes: NASA	40
Video game designer	42
Behind the scenes: Video game company	44
Glossary	46
Index	48

Top math jobs

Who needs math? The answer to this question is . . . everyone! We all use math in our everyday lives, whether it is to work on your homework or to keep the score in a sports game. At work, basic math skills are needed in most jobs. There is only really one way to learn math and that is through practice. Get into the habit of practicing math problems and you will find that you can improve very quickly.

STUDYING MATHEMATICS

At school, math is a compulsory subject and you should study it hard whatever you want to do in the future, as all employers value good math qualifications. Studying math not only makes you good at doing sums, it also trains you to think logically and to analyze problems. As well as the jobs listed in this book, math is an essential part of all science, technology, and engineering jobs.

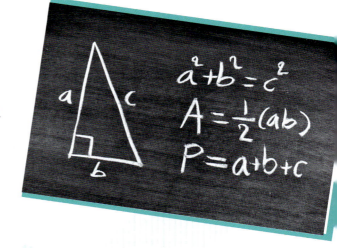

WHAT IS A MODEL?

Mathematics is a great tool for creating models. A model is a representation of an object or system using numbers. These numbers can be fed into a computer in order to analyze them. For instance, mathematical models of Earth's atmosphere allow scientists to track weather systems and create weather forecasts.

MATH IS BEAUTIFUL

Many mathematicians believe that math is extremely beautiful. It provides the key to understanding some of the deepest mysteries in sciences, such as physics and biology, as well as the patterns found in art and music. Ours is a mathematical universe, whose patterns and systems all have structures that can be described using numbers.

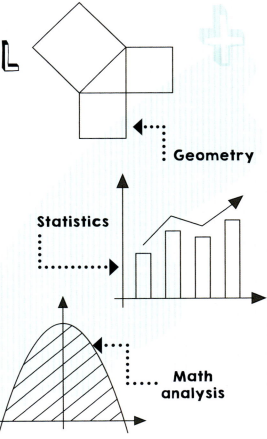

Geometry

Statistics

Math analysis

5

Computer programmer

Do you enjoy messing around with computer code? Math skills come in very handy for computer programmers. Code needs to be written in a clear, logical way so that the computer does exactly what you want it to do. If you're good at math, you could be great at coding.

COMPUTER MODELS

Coders often find themselves creating code for computer models. These are programs that simulate an object, such as a building, a landscape, or a machine. The models allow you to take a virtual tour on-screen around the object. The models may even be projected in three dimensions so that you can walk through them. Programmers use math to make sure the models look just right.

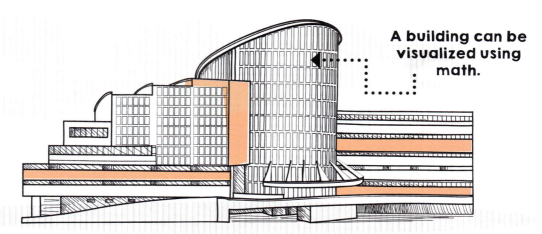

A building can be visualized using math.

TESTING SOFTWARE

The programs that run on computers are called software. Before new software goes into operation, it needs to be thoroughly tested. Testing software requires imagination as you'll need to do your best to break it, probing it for weaknesses. When you find problems, you'll need to check the code and come up with suggested solutions.

STEM STAR: ADA LOVELACE
(1815–1852)

British mathematician Ada Lovelace was one of the first people to see the potential of computers. When her friend and fellow mathematician Charles Babbage (1791–1871) showed Lovelace his design for a computing machine made from gears, she understood that it could do far more than sums. She saw that it could also be used to create many other things, such as music, and she sketched out programs to run on it. The computer programming language Ada is named in her honor.

Cryptographer

Do you spend hours solving number puzzles, such as Sudoku? You might be cut out for working in cryptography, which is the creation and breaking of secret codes. Cryptography is crucial in today's high-tech world, as it allows us to send information to each other safely. Cryptographers also work for intelligence agencies, trying to break the codes made by criminals.

SAFETY NET

Whenever you send a message on the internet, other people might try to intercept it and steal information, such as your bank details. Cryptographers keep your information safe using mathematics. They use special numbers—called prime numbers—to turn your information into a secret code that only the person or company you are sending it to can decipher.

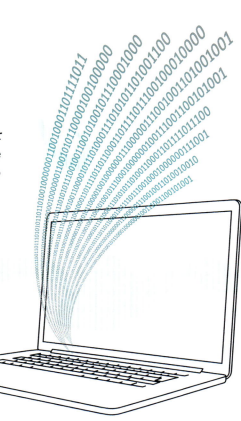

STEM STAR: ALAN TURING
(1912-1954)

During the Second World War (1939–1945), mathematician Alan Turing led a team of British cryptographers that broke the secret codes made by the German navy who used Enigma encryption machines. This achievement has been credited with shortening the war by up to two years. Turing was also a pioneer in computer science. He was the first to design a computer that stores programs in its memory, an idea that is the basis of all modern computing.

CODE BREAKERS

Cryptographers are both expert code makers and code breakers. You'll need to be great at solving hard number puzzles in order to design and test your codes. Cryptographers spend much of their time trying to break existing systems, probing them for potential weak spots. It takes superior math skills and imagination to come up with solutions that nobody else has thought of.

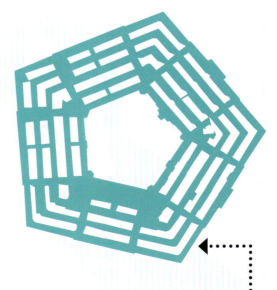

The Pentagon in Washington, D.C., is the home of the Department of Defense, which uses some of the world's most complex secret codes.

Meteorologist

Do you moan when weather forecasters get it wrong and you're soaked by an unexpected shower? If you think you can do better, you could become a meteorologist. These are scientists who study Earth's atmosphere and predict how the weather will change. It's not an easy job, but equipped with cutting-edge technology, forecasters are getting better at it all the time.

MAKING MODELS

Meteorologists predict the weather using mathematical models. These are computer programs that take information about the current state of the atmosphere, such as measurements from weather stations and satellites, and work out how the weather systems are likely to develop. Huge amounts of data are collected and the numbers are crunched using some of the most powerful computers in the world.

STEM STAR: EDWARD LORENZ
(1917-2008)

American meteorologist Edward Lorenz developed a field of mathematics called chaos theory, which describes how very different weather can be produced by changing the conditions just a tiny bit. This is now often described as "the Butterfly Effect," meaning that the swish of the wings of a butterfly might change the conditions of the atmosphere in such a way that it causes a hurricane on the other side of the world. As a result of Lorenz's work, meteorologists now produce a range of different possibilities in their forecasts, recognizing that they cannot say for sure which one will happen.

Meteorologists try to predict the paths and strengths of hurricanes.

CLIMATE CHANGE

As well as predicting the weather, meteorologists also monitor long-term changes in the atmosphere, which are causing climate change. In the 1970s, scientists began to suspect that human activity, such as releasing carbon dioxide into the atmosphere by burning fossil fuels, was causing Earth to warm up. By the 1990s, they had conclusive proof that global warming was happening. We are now increasing our use of renewable energy sources, such as wind and solar, to try and reduce the release of greenhouse gases and slow down global warming.

Behind the scenes: Climate scientists

In addition to creating weather forecasts, meteorologists and climate scientists study long-term changes and patterns in the weather, which form the world's climates. Understanding how the climate is changing is vital to ensure that we can limit global warming.

MODELING THE FUTURE

The Met Office Hadley Centre for Climate Change, based in Exeter, United Kingdom, is one of the world's leading centers for climate change study. Scientists at the Hadley Centre work with other organizations around the world to develop mathematical models to calculate what might happen in the future, depending on how much we change our fossil fuel use.

Scientists believe that emissions released by coal-fired power stations are a significant cause of climate change.

STUDYING THE PAST

To understand how the climate might change in the future, scientists study how it has changed in the past. This can involve fieldwork in faraway places, extracting ice cores from deep under the ice caps in the Arctic or sediment from the bottom of the oceans. The material in these samples is thousands of years old and contains layers of minerals and chemicals that tell us what the climate was like when the layers formed. In this way, scientists build a detailed picture of how the climate has changed over the last few thousand years.

Research camp in Antarctica

SOUTH POLE STATION

If you want an extreme posting, how about working at the Amundsen-Scott Station at the South Pole? Here, scientists collect information on temperature, wind, and air pressure in the lower and upper atmosphere. This data is hugely important both for weather forecasters and climate change scientists. Researchers live at the base for months at a time, where temperatures can drop to -80°F (-62°C) and can feel even colder.

The base at the American Amundsen-Scott South Pole Station

13

Research mathematician

Are you regularly top of the class in math? Research mathematicians are high-flying thinkers who come up with new mathematical ideas. To become a research mathematician, you need to have a real flair for numbers. You also need to be prepared to put in some serious work. Advanced mathematics is hard!

CASH PRIZES

While research mathematicians do what they do because they love it, some also work on the solutions to problems that come with a big cash reward. These are puzzles that have stumped mathematicians for many years. One of the most famous is called the Riemann Hypothesis, which has remained unsolved since 1859. You'll pocket a cool $1 million if you can solve it!

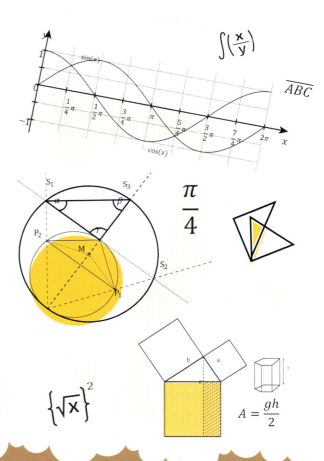

WEIRD MATH

When he was writing the equations for his general theory of relativity, published in 1916, physicist Albert Einstein (1879–1955) worked closely with research mathematicians. They helped correct some of the errors in his math. Today, mathematicians often work closely with physicists, formulating the equations that describe strange objects, such as black holes.

Black holes are regions of space where the gravity is so strong that not even light can escape.

STEM STAR: MARYAM MIRZAKHANI (1977-2017)

Iranian mathematician Maryam Mirzakhani was one of the most brilliant minds of her generation. She worked in the field of geometry, studying the properties of curved surfaces. In 2014, Mirzakhani became the first woman to win the Fields Medal, the top prize in mathematics.

Maryam Mirzakhani at the International Congress of Mathematicians in 2014

Statistician

Experiments are at the heart of all good science. Scientists carry out experiments to test their theories about how the world works. But they need to know exactly what the results of the experiments mean. Do the results support their theories or not? This is where statisticians come in, providing the mathematical tools needed to make sense of the numbers.

GETTING RESULTS

Statisticians analyze the results of experiments to determine whether those results are "statistically significant." This is a measure of how likely the result is to have happened simply by chance. For instance, experimenters need to know if the results of a drug trial show that the drug is effective. If the drug causes a statistically significant improvement in people's health, then it may be worth mass producing. If not, then a new drug will need to be developed.

STEM STAR: GERTRUDE COX (1900–1978)

In 1950, U.S. statistician Gertrude Cox wrote a book called *Experimental Design* with her colleague William Cochran. It has become a classic work in science. The book explains how to design experiments that can be repeated and are reliable. The ability to repeat experiments is crucial to science as it allows other scientists to check your results.

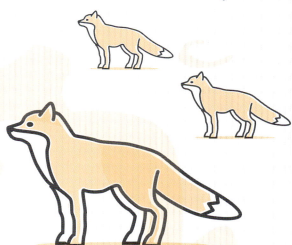

FOXES AND RABBITS

Populations of animals or plants can go up and down wildly over time. Mathematicians use a branch of math called game theory to work out why this might be. Game theory describes populations that are in conflict or competition with one another. For instance, if a population of rabbits goes down, that might be because there are lots of foxes around to eat them. Then, the shortage in the number of rabbits will cause a crash in the numbers of foxes, which in turn will allow the rabbit population to increase again.

17

Opinion pollster

Are you into politics? At election time, do you follow the polls and try to work out what is going to happen? Pollsters carry out surveys of thousands of people and analyze the results. They use these results to try to predict how millions of people will vote in the election. It is important to get this right. Few politicians will act before they have checked the polls.

CHECKING GROUPS

To be an effective pollster, you need to be skilled in a wide range of things, including math, geography, and psychology. You need to select a range of people to interview who represent the wider population fairly in terms of, for example, age, sex, wealth, and ethnicity. You also need to look at past data to work out who, out of those you are interviewing, is actually likely to vote.

STEM STAR: NATE SILVER
(1978–)

U.S. statistician Nate Silver runs a website dedicated to opinion poll analysis called FiveThirtyEight. He uses math to create new ways to make polling data more accurate. Using his system, Silver correctly predicted the polling result in every U.S. state during the 2012 presidential election.

SURVEYING ATTITUDES

As well as finding out how people are going to vote, pollsters also ask a wide range of questions about their wider concerns. Politicians use this information to work out which policies are likely to be popular. Surveys conducted after an election provide information about why people voted as they did, showing which campaign strategies were effective.

Sports analyst

Do you love sports stats? Can you quote a player's batting average or goal-scoring record off the top of your head? You might love a job as a sports analyst. Today, top teams in many different sports employ analysts, whose job it is to crunch the data to reveal new facts about the team's performance.

SABERMETRICS

Statistical analysis is probably used in baseball more than in any other sport. A sophisticated system called sabermetrics has been developed to assess the performances of players. This measures not only the number of runs scored by a batter or given away by a pitcher, but also how particular players fare against one another or how they help their team.

STEM STAR: BILLY BEANE (1962–)

Billy Beane shot to fame in 2002 as manager of the Oakland Athletics baseball team. With a very limited budget, Beane put together a winning team using advanced sabermetrics to identify players who had been undervalued by other teams. In 2011, the story of their successful season was made into the film *Moneyball*. Following Beane's example, sabermetrics is now widely used in many sports.

COACHING AIDS

Sports analysts play an important role in guiding a player's training and fitness. Using slow-motion video, they can pinpoint the likely stresses on the player's body and recommend changes in their technique where they think this is necessary. In this way, players can avoid injury, improve their performance and prolong their careers.

PLAYER PERFORMANCE

In the top professional leagues, almost every aspect of a football player's performance is measured, including how far they run during a game, the areas they run to, the number of times they touch the ball, the accuracy of their passes, and even their heart rate. Analysts use this data to help players and coaches analyze their performance. They also use data on opposition players to work out the best tactics to use against them.

Behind the scenes: Hawk-Eye

Would you like to fly around the world covering major sports events? That's what you do when you work for companies like Hawk-Eye, which provides instant replays and analysis in sports, such as tennis, cricket, and baseball. You can put your mathematical skills to great use making sure the images are correct.

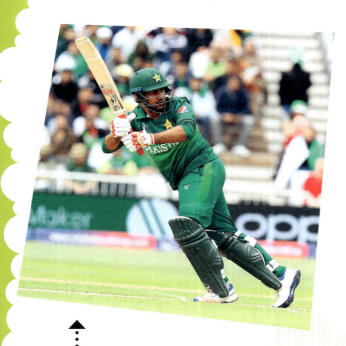

Major cricket matches use Hawk-Eye to check and even overrule umpire decisions.

HOW IT WORKS

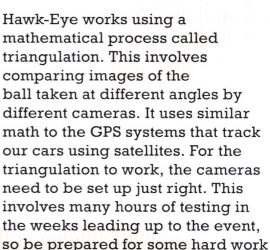

Hawk-Eye works using a mathematical process called triangulation. This involves comparing images of the ball taken at different angles by different cameras. It uses similar math to the GPS systems that track our cars using satellites. For the triangulation to work, the cameras need to be set up just right. This involves many hours of testing in the weeks leading up to the event, so be prepared for some hard work long before the action starts.

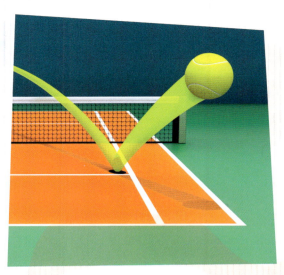

DECISION REVIEW

In tennis and cricket, players can challenge the decisions made by umpires by asking to look at a Hawk-Eye replay. In tennis, the replay shows whether the ball landed in or out of the court. In cricket, it tracks the path of the ball and helps determine whether a batsman should be given out. Hawk-Eye also provides pictures for TV viewers, showing information such as serving speeds in tennis.

This tennis Hawk-Eye replay shows that the ball bounced inside the court.

TRAINING TOOL

As well as helping officials to make the correct decisions in games, high-tech camera systems such as Hawk-Eye are a great tool for coaches. Shot analysis shows the accuracy of a player's shots, the spin on the ball, and the path each shot takes. Coaches can set their players targets and Hawk-Eye will show exactly how well they are doing in achieving those targets.

Hawk-Eye is used to show the path of a baseball pitch.

23

Roboticist

Robots are machines that move and make decisions on their own. You need to understand mathematics to develop robots, which in turn use math to work out what to do next. Mathematicians develop the programs to crunch the numbers and also create clever computer code to make robots that can learn for themselves.

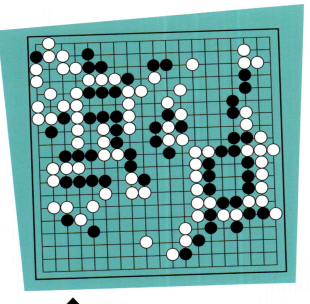

Go was invented in China more than 2,500 years ago.

GO CHAMPION

Smart robots that can work out new strategies are said to have artificial intelligence (AI). In 2017, an AI computer program called AlphaGo beat Ke Jie (1997–), the world's best player of the board game Go. A strategy board game, Go had been thought by many people to be too complex ever to be mastered by a machine. AlphaGo was first trained by learning from 160,000 different historic games. It then improved its strategies by playing millions of games against itself. Ke Jie later studied the computer's strategies and used them to improve his own game.

BIONIC LIMBS

Do you want to create a bionic human being? Once the stuff of science fiction, artificial arms and legs controlled by the mind are now a reality. They are connected to nerves in a person's body, which allows their brain to send signals to the limbs. With training, people become able to move the limbs as if they were their own!

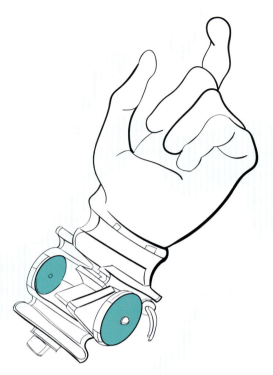

STEM STAR: DANIELA RUS (1963–)

Roboticist Daniela Rus is the Director of the Computer Science and Artificial Intelligence Laboratory at the Massachusetts Institute of Technology (MIT). Rus develops robots that work and learn next to humans, such as robotic vehicles and robots that help people with disabilities in their homes. She also designed a robot that could follow whales across the ocean, catching previously unknown behavior on film.

Behind the scenes: Robotics lab

Robotics labs are high-tech places where scientists develop new robotic technology. They build models called prototypes and test them out with a variety of tasks. Mathematicians, engineers, and computer programmers develop robots of all shapes and sizes, from tiny robotic bees to giant robotic arms for use on space stations.

VIRTUAL ROBOTS

Soon, you could be controlling robots in your math classes! U.S. robotics firm RobotLab brings robots into the classroom via virtual reality. Programmers create virtual 3D worlds and hook them up to real-life robots. This allows students to control the robots from the classroom via the internet, using math calculations to make the robots move and to check the results.

SOFT ROBOTS

When you imagine what robots look like, do you think of clunky metal machines? Many robots of the future will look very different from this. Soft robots are made of flexible, elastic materials, which allow them to move more like living creatures. Some are made to look like animals. Scientists in Japan have made a robotic snake that can slither its way up ladders.

Snake robots can access places that are harder to reach for "normal" walking robots.

SPACE ROBOTS

NASA regularly sends robots into space. Robots can work in dangerous places that humans cannot go and they don't have to be brought back to Earth when their work is done! Working with scientists at Stanford University's robotics lab, NASA has made a robot that looks like a spiky cube, called Hedgehog. It will be sent to explore small bodies in space, such as asteroids and comets. Instead of rolling, Hedgehog hops and tumbles over rough terrain to prevent it from getting stuck. It can even blast itself out of deep craters if it falls in.

NASA's Hedgehog roving robot

27

Theme park designer

Have you ever ridden on a rollercoaster and wondered exactly how you didn't fall out? The secret is in the math. Theme parks are always on the lookout for fresh ways to thrill people, and they employ teams of designers to develop them. You'll need to get creative with your calculations to come up with something safe and exciting.

SAFE THRILLS

The rides at a theme park are actually less dangerous than they feel. When you are designing a new ride, you need to use math to calculate the forces that people will be placed under. For instance, at the top of a loop-the-loop, the car needs to be going fast enough for people to stay safely pinned to their seats. The trick is to make something that is really very safe feel terrifying!

STEM STAR: JOHN WARDLEY (1950–)

The Smiler rollercoaster at Alton Towers in England, which opened in 2013, includes 14 inversions. This means that it turns you upside down 14 times during a ride, more than any other ride in the world. It was the brainchild of designer John Wardley. Over his long career, Wardley built a number of award-winning rollercoasters. He also created the special effects for five James Bond films.

.... The Smiler rollercoaster

SMOOTH RUNNING

In addition to exciting rides, a theme park needs to be a well-organized place. People need to be able to get from one part of the park to another easily and safely. Park designers use math to work out how to create the most pleasant visitor experience. They identify the busiest areas and work out how to keep so many people moving, helping to avoid long and frustrating lines.

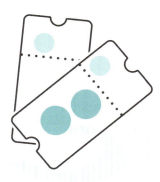

Urban planner

Do you enjoy creating your own towns out of building bricks? Urban planners do this for real. Around the world, more people than ever are choosing to live in towns and cities. Urban planners use math to make sure everyone in an urban area has a place to live with everything they need in easy reach.

GREEN CITIES

New cities need to be as green as possible so that people don't use too much energy. Planners create bicycle routes and walking paths alongside roads to give a clean alternative to the car. In many cities, people can rent bikes on the street. Planners mix built-up areas with lots of green spaces for people to relax in and to help keep the air clean.

STEM STAR: NIKOS SALINGAROS (1952–)

Greek mathematician Nikos Salingaros uses a branch of mathematics called fractal geometry to plan cities. He sees cities as giant networks made up of lots of smaller areas connecting together to form larger areas. Salingaros believes that this kind of planning allows people to live together in huge cities without feeling overwhelmed by them.

TRAFFIC PLANNING

Rush-hour traffic can clog up cities in the mornings and evenings as everyone is traveling to or from work or school. Planners collect data to tell them which routes are used the most. They put this information into computers to work out the best way to keep the trains and traffic running smoothly. Their aim is to make sure that everyone gets home as quickly and safely as possible.

Fraud investigator

Do you enjoy playing number puzzles and solving mysteries? Fraud investigators get to do both of these things at once. They spot strange patterns in the numbers in accounts that mean someone might be stealing money. Follow the money and catch the crooks!

CRACKING COMPUTER CRIME

Many crimes today are committed on computers. Digital forensics investigators track down wrongdoing by retrieving information from computer hard drives. They also collect evidence from smartphones and social media. As a digital forensics investigator, you could find yourself working for courts, private companies, or the intelligence services.

STEM STAR: HARRY MARKOPOLOS (1956–)

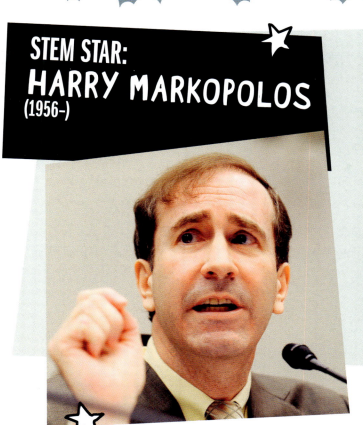

American fraud investigator Harry Markopolos uncovered the biggest financial fraud in history when he revealed that New York hedge fund manager Bernard Madoff (1938–2021) was stealing from his clients. Markopolos had been asked to find out why Madoff was so successful. He realized that Madoff's huge profits were impossible, meaning that he had to be cheating. Investors lost billions of dollars in Madoff's fraud, which was revealed in 2009. He was sentenced to 150 years in prison.

COMPANY FRAUD

Not all crime is committed by individuals. In some cases, companies act illegally by declaring false profits or underfunding their pension plans. Fraud investigators study company accounts to make sure they are correct. If you find something wrong, you will need to build a case that can be taken to court.

33

Cartographer

Have you ever wondered how the maps on a smartphone work? They are made by cartographers, who gather information from a wide range of sources, including land surveys, satellite images, and aerial photography, to create accurate maps.

MAKING MAPS

Today's maps are created using computers. Cartographers need to decide what information to include on their maps. For instance, a road map may not include information about hills, but a map for walkers certainly will. Once they have decided what to include, they gather the information and feed it into the computer.

CREATING PROJECTIONS

If you compare a map to a globe, you will see that they look different. This is because it is impossible to accurately represent the spherical surface of Earth on a flat map. Cartographers use mathematics to create projections that turn the curved surface into a flat one, but all projections create distortions. For instance, maps of the world often use the Mercator projection. This creates parallel lines of latitude, but makes places near the poles appear much bigger, so that Greenland appears many times larger than it actually is.

MEASURING EXACTLY

We all know that Earth is roughly a giant sphere in shape, but its exact shape is slightly different. For instance, it is squashed at the poles. It also changes shape slightly over time as the plates in Earth's crust move around. Geodesists measure the shape of the planet and how it is changing. Cartographers use this information to improve their maps, and it is also needed to produce accurate satellite positioning systems, such as the ones used by satnav.

STEM STAR: ARNO PETERS (1916-2002)

Dissatisfied with the Mercator projection, German historian Arno Peters created the Peters world map in 1974. Peters was concerned that the Mercator projection represented countries in richer parts of the world, such as Europe and North America, as much bigger than they really are, while countries in developing parts of the world, such as Africa, were much smaller. On the Peters projection, each continent is the correct area, although its shape is distorted.

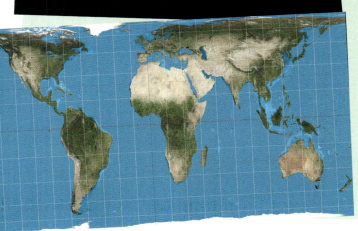

A Peters projection of the world

Space scientist

Have you ever wondered how space probes find their way to other planets? Guiding rockets through space requires a lot of mathematics. Space scientists use math to calculate the paths spacecraft need to take in order to reach their destinations.

SLINGSHOT

To speed them along their way, spacecraft destined for distant planets are given boosts called gravitational slingshots. These use the gravity of nearby planets to fling the craft towards their destination. For instance, the Voyager 1 space probe flew close to Saturn in 1981, and this had the effect of slinging it towards Uranus, which it reached five years later. Space scientists study the positions of the planets to time the arrival of their spacecraft perfectly so that the slingshots send them off in exactly the right direction.

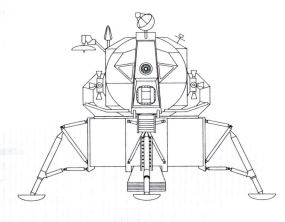

HUMAN COMPUTERS

Today, computers are high-tech machines that make calculations at incredible speed. But before the machines, computers were human beings. Teams of computers worked for NASA in the 1950s, doing the math needed to make space flight possible using only pen and paper. Many of these human computers were women, chosen for their superb ability with sums. Working long hours for low pay, they were the unsung heroes of the U.S. space program.

STEM STAR: MARY JACKSON
(1921-2005)

U.S. mathematician Mary Jackson began her career as a human computer for NASA's space program. She took engineering classes in her free time and became NASA's first black female engineer in 1958. She carried out research in the field of aerodynamics, studying the way objects move at high speed. Later in her career, Jackson campaigned to help other women begin careers in science, mathematics, and technology.

Astronomer

Do you stare at the night sky and wonder what might be out there? It is an astronomer's job to find out. Astronomers use math all the time, whether calculating the distance of stars, finding new planets, or discovering odd objects, such as quasars and black holes.

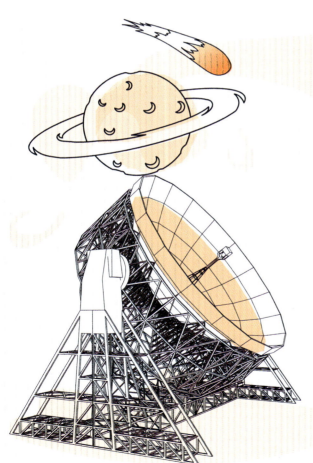

NUMBER CRUNCHING

The biggest modern telescopes are so powerful that they could see a human hair from more than 30 miles (50 km) away! Cameras record the information captured by the telescopes and turn it into numbers. This is where math comes in. The numbers represent the strength and kind of light being given off by objects in the sky. Astronomers put the numbers into a computer and crunch them (carry out a large number of calculations) to work out what the objects might be and how they are moving.

PLANET HUNTERS

Even with the most powerful telescopes, stars are so distant that they look like points of light in the sky. Nevertheless, astronomers have worked out ways to find planets in orbit around them. Planet hunters look for a wobble in the star's position caused by the gravity of planets in orbit around them, or detect tiny changes in the star's brightness as a planet passes in front of it. They have discovered thousands of planets orbiting distant stars. One of them may be just like Earth and contain life!

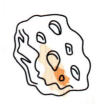
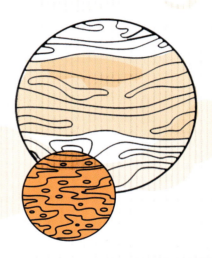

STEM STAR: URBAIN LE VERRIER
(1811–1877)

The planet Neptune was discovered in 1846 using math. The orbit of the planet Uranus had a strange shape that suggested it was being pulled by the gravity of another planet. French mathematician Urbain le Verrier used math to calculate where the other planet should be, allowing astronomers to point their telescopes in exactly the right direction to find it.

39

Behind the scenes: NASA

NASA is the biggest space agency in the world, and it employs thousands of people. A lucky few get to go into space, but if you are good at math, there are plenty of opportunities at NASA that don't involve putting on a spacesuit. Often you will be working alongside the leading experts in their fields, developing projects that open up new frontiers in space exploration.

SPACE MATH

Thousands of scientists and mathematicians are employed by NASA to carry out groundbreaking research into a wide range of areas, from planetary science and the physics of stars to water purification techniques and medical advances. You could be helping design instruments that will probe the sun or studying the health of the crew on the International Space Station (ISS).

Astronauts can spend several months at a time on the ISS.

NEW TELESCOPE

One of NASA's biggest current projects is the James Webb Space Telescope (JWST). Launched into orbit in 2021, the telescope is designed to explore the universe by detecting infrared light and provide detailed views of the objects in our solar system as well as images of very distant galaxies. The engineers building the JWST had to get their measurements precisely right, so that its hexagonal gold-plated mirrors collect and focus the light correctly.

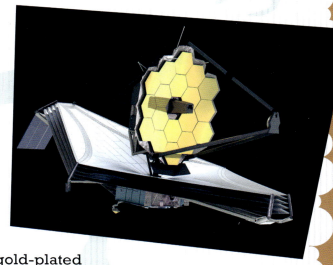

RETURN TO THE MOON

A human last walked on the surface of the moon in 1972. After more than 50 years away, NASA plans to return to the moon around 2025, while China is considering a crewed mission to the moon in the 2030s. NASA's projects also look far into the future, planning what might be possible in 20 or 30 years' time. Space scientists are also working on projects to put humans on Mars.

An artist's impression of a moon lander.

41

Video game designer

Are you often being scolded for spending too much time playing video games? Why not try your hand at making them? Gaming is a huge industry today, with billions of players around the world. To design a video game, you'll need the skill of a mathematician and the imagination of an artist.

DESIGN TEAMS

Big teams of designers work on each game. Environmental designers create the imaginary worlds in which games are set. A game mechanics designer develops the rules to make sure they work fairly. Story designers create characters and plots for the game. In overall control is a lead designer, who, like the director of a film, makes sure everything comes together.

MATHEMATICAL WORLDS

Math is the secret behind all video games. Without it, characters would not be able to walk up a slope, fire a weapon, or jump up and down. The forces that make us move, such as gravity, which pulls objects to the ground, need to be turned into math to make the games work. The stunning 3D graphics systems that create realistic-looking worlds also use mathematics to make sure everything looks just right as you move around.

STEM STAR: SATOSHI TAJIRI (1965–)

Japanese video game fanatic Satoshi Tajiri taught himself how to write computer code in order to make his own games. In the 1990s, Tajiri developed the Pokémon video game, which later became a wildly popular card-trading game too. Today, Pokémon is a large media franchise, including video games, movies, and anime and manga cartoons.

Pikachu is one of the main Pokémon characters.

Behind the scenes: Video game company

A great video game creates an entire virtual universe for players to move around in. This takes a huge amount of work. The multiplayer fantasy adventure game *World of Warcraft* was created by U.S. video game developer Blizzard Entertainment. It took five years to develop and is regularly updated. A team of artists, coders, writers, and computer scientists works hard to keep the game fresh and running smoothly.

Players can choose which character to play as.

SKILL LEVELS

Like most video games, *World of Warcraft* was set up with different skill levels. As players became more experienced, they unlocked more challenging levels within the game. Programmers use mathematical formulas to calculate when a player should move up a level. However, Blizzard Entertainment soon had to change the calculations. Many players were reaching the maximum skill level and finding themselves with nothing more to do. In response, Blizzard created new, even harder levels for the most advanced players to unlock.

EXPANSION

As *World of Warcraft* grew in popularity, Blizzard added new powers to keep fans stimulated. One of their biggest challenges came with the addition of flying mounts. These were powers that allowed advanced players to fly high above the scenery. The original world had not been designed to be seen from above, so the programmers had to add new angles from which to view each landscape, using math to create a realistic change in perspective as the players flew around the digital world.

The game features many fantastical creatures, including orcs.

FIXING BUGS

Before a game is released, it has to be thoroughly tested for bugs. These are mistakes in the coding that make things go wrong in the game. Testers play the game all the way through, noting any mistakes. Once a bug has been detected, programmers must go back into the code and fix it. Often, bugs are only detected by players after the game has been released. Players contact the company, who fix the bug and send out an update.

Companies reveal new games and additions at trade fairs around the world.

45

Glossary

aerodynamics
the study of how objects move through the air

air pressure
the force of the atmosphere pushing down on an area. Air pressure can vary with height and as the temperature changes as the air gets warmer or colder.

artificial intelligence
a type of computer technology where computers and machines work and act in an intelligent way, learning to improve from different tasks they are given

black hole
a region of space where the force of gravity is so strong that nothing can escape it, not even light

bug
an error in a piece of computer code that stops the code from working correctly

cartographer
a person who designs and creates maps

chaos theory
a branch of science where apparently random events are linked by a single theory

climate
the weather conditions that occur in a region over a period of time. Climate conditions vary around the globe, depending on a wide range of factors, such as a region's latitude (its distance from the equator), its distance from the sea, and its altitude.

compulsory
refers to something that must be done, either because it is the law or because someone in authority has told you to do it

computer code
this is the language in which a series of instructions, called a program, is given to a computer telling it what to do

cryptography
the studying, creating, and breaking of codes

data
a collection of information, including facts, figures, measurements, and observations

decipher
to translate a secret message or code into a language that is easy to understand

fossil fuel
fuel formed from the remains of long-dead plants and animals that lived millions of years ago. Fossil fuels include coal, oil, gas, and peat.

game theory
a mathematical theory that studies different strategies and choices in situations where there is conflict

geodesist
a scientist who works out the exact location of places on Earth as well as the planet's exact size and shape

global warming
the gradual rise in Earth's temperature caused by an increase in levels of carbon dioxide and other greenhouse gases

GPS
short for Global Positioning System, this is a network of satellites in orbit around Earth whose signals are used to pinpoint a position on or above the planet

hard drive
the part of a computer on which data is written, stored, and read

ice caps
a large expanse of ice, for example across Earth's polar regions

ice core
a cylindrical sample of ice that contains ice from a range of years, with recently formed ice in the top layers and older ice in lower layers

loop-the-loop
to fly or travel in a complete vertical circle

meteorologist
a scientist who studies Earth's atmosphere and the weather conditions it produces

NASA
short for National Aeronautics and Space Administration, the organization that runs the U.S. space exploration program

prime numbers
whole numbers that are greater than 1 and can only be divided exactly by 1 and themselves

programmer
a person who writes computer programs using computer languages or codes

projection
a representation of a three-dimensional shape onto a two-dimensional surface. A world map is a projection of the entire Earth on a flat surface.

qualifications
an achievement of successfully completing a course or an exam

software
instructions followed by a computer when it is doing tasks

sphere
a three-dimensional object that is completely round in shape

survey
information about a group of people or an area that is usually collected using a number of questions

three dimensions
also known as 3D, this refers to something that has height, width, and depth

triangulation
finding the exact location of a point by taking bearings from two other points and seeing where they meet

umpire
a person who oversees some competitions to make sure they are played fairly, that no rules are broken, and to judge on certain decisions. Umpires are used in sports such as baseball and tennis.

urban planners
people who design and plan urban areas, such as towns and cities, and decide on the style of buildings and the balance of different land uses, such as industrial and open spaces

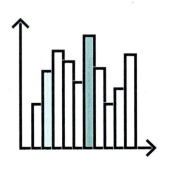

Index

Amundsen-Scott Station 13
artificial intelligence (AI) 24
astronomers 38–39

Babbage, Charles 7
Beane, Billy 21
beauty of math 5
bionics 25
black holes 15
Butterfly Effect 11

cartographers 34–35
chaos theory 11
climate scientists 11, 12–13
Cochran, William 17
code breakers 9
coding 6
computer programmers 6–7
Cox, Gertrude 17
cryptographers 8–9

digital forensics investigators 32

Einstein, Albert 15
experiment design 17

Fields Medal 15
fractal geometry 31
fraud investigators 32–33

game theory 17
geodesists 35
Go board game 24
gravitational slingshots 36
green cities 30

Hawk-Eye 22–23
human computers 37

Jackson, Mary 37
James Webb Space Telescope (JWST) 41

le Verrier, Urbain 39
Lorenz, Edward 11
Lovelace, Ada 7

maps and globes 34–35
Markopolos, Harry 33
Mercator projection 34, 35
meteorologists 10–11, 12, 13
Mirzakhani, Maryam 15
models 5, 6, 10, 12
moon missions 41

NASA 27, 37, 40–41
number crunching 10, 20, 24, 38

opinion pollsters 18–19

Peters, Arno 35
Peters projection 35
planet-hunters 39
prime numbers 8

Riemann Hypothesis 14
research mathematicians 14–15
roboticists 24–27
rollercoasters 29
Rus, Daniela 25

sabermetrics 20, 21
Salingaros, Nikos 31
school, studying math at 4

Silver, Nate 19
software testing 7
space robots 27
space scientists 36–37, 40–41
sports analysts 20–23
statisticians 16–17

Tajiri, Satoshi 43
theme park designers 28–29
traffic planning 31
triangulation 22
Turing, Alan 9

urban planners 30–31

video game designers 42–45
virtual reality 26

Wardley, John 29
weather forecasting 10–11, 13
World of Warcraft 44–45

48